CW01459611

RESILIENT GRIEVING AND
STRENGTHS OF HER

Resilient Grieving and Strengths of Her

RENEE GARRETT

PALMETTO
PUBLISHING
Charleston, SC
www.PalmettoPublishing.com

Hardcover ISBN: 9798822956520
Paperback ISBN: 9798822956537

Each day is a new beginning. We can always put the past behind us and look toward the future. We can learn from the past; it can be a blessing or a lesson. How you start your day depends on you. There can be a number of factors that can shift it. We never know how it will end until it's in our presence. There are some days when you just want to stay home, relax, and chill, but there are days you just want to spend time with loved ones, friends, and family. There are just some days that you don't understand why life is the way it is and the situations that are beyond your control.

Every Saturday morning I call my best friend, Shawntel, to go out for brunch to our favorite espresso shop. Shawntel is the type of girl who loves the outdoors and going out for good food and drinks. She's the type where she'll get up at 3:00 a.m. and go sit by the water and chill. I can always depend on her. Even when Shawntel had a boyfriend named Jorbin, she still always made time for her friends and family.

Jorbin was always kind of weird to me though. I've always supported and respected Shawntel's decisions, but when she met Jorbin, she thought she had met the man of her dreams. Shawntel and I had disagreements in the past, but we would always bounce back and move on.

Shawntel and I have been on several cruises. We've been to Jamaica, the Bahamas, the Cayman Islands, and Key West, Florida; this is just to name a few. We've been to so many places, and each time we went, we always had such an amazing time.

Shawntel and I were sitting out on a beautiful Saturday evening just watching everyone enjoy themselves. We met this guy who was so down-to-earth. He was not a shy person at all. He would dance to whatever music that came on and just go for it. He would come out in costumes and shake it like a tail feather.

We would get him so pumped up because we enjoyed his dancing. We labeled him as "celebrity." Every time he danced, we would say, "Celebrity,

Celebrity, Celebrity," and he would just suck it up. We would hype this dude up.

The next morning it was time for breakfast. He sat with Shawntel and I, and we just had such a good time. Soon as the music came on, the celebrity ran back out to the stage, and he got the crowd hyped. We pumped him up again and said, "Celebrity, Celebrity, Celebrity." He thought he was a celebrity. The next morning, we saw him. He acted like he didn't even know us. He thought he was a true celebrity.

We were just playing and having a good time, but he took it seriously, to this day we do not know what happened to Mr. Celebrity.

To be honest he made our day. Our vacation was worth it. Just enjoying and having such an amazing time was everything. Shawntel was pregnant and didn't know it at the time; meanwhile I started my period, and all this took place while cruising. Isn't that something?

I've had a few relationships in the past, and they've never turned out the way I've wanted them to be. Let's just say, it wasn't me; it was the man I'd chosen who I thought was for me, but I kept one of them longer than I expected. He was almost there, but not quite there. I'll give him four stars, but it would have been perfect at five stars. I have standards, and there was no way I was going to ever settle for less than. When you're young and nowadays even older, you still try to make relationships work. Our selfish ways can also be very challenging, but at the end of the day, it is what they are.

Shawntel and I became good friends in elementary school. We would do everything together. We would take long walks and pick blackberries, pears, plums, sweetgrass, figs, sugarcane, and even drink water out of the water hose. We would dress up in our mothers' high heels, put on their wigs and makeup, and pretend we were going to the disco club. Those were the good ole days! How could you ever forget something like that? Shawntel was the smart one, but let's just say, I was not too far from behind her. I got an F in social studies, and I knew I was going to get in trouble, so what did Ms. Shawntel do? She said,

"Savannah, just change it to a B." And so, I did! It was golden to make it look like I made the honor roll. I would have never thought of such a thing like that. Of course, Shawntel would! She always had on her thinking cap.

Shawntel and I did some crazy things together. We would run underneath the train with our cousins, but of course I was the scared one, me and my cousin named Wanda. Our aunt Lindsey always wanted Shawntel and I to do the dishes. When everybody went to sleep at her grandmother's house, we would sneak and eat cold cornbread out the fridge. We used to climb the pipes on the side of her grandmother's house to get on top of the house to hide. But of course, we would get caught every time because my aunt would always hear me breathing hard or crying for some odd reason. Shawntel would climb the trees and tumble down and hit every branch. She would climb the tree, throw pears, and shake the pecan trees. She was a tough one. If you dared her to do something, she would do it. She would get up and try it again, like nothing ever happened. She was insane.

Growing up together as best friends, we have done everything together. We have had some good days and some bad days, but we always seemed to get through the good times and bad times together no matter what they were. We never grew apart even though we both had our own separate lives. With her raising her children in a different state, we still communicated when schedules permitted us to do so. Shawntel's heart was so full of love and gold. She was very outgoing, genuine, extroverted, but at times could also be a little introverted, nice, and would give you the world. She would coach me through my anxiety attacks and teach me how to breathe and let me know it would be ok. She used to experience that same thing. She would always tell me, "You got this best friend." The only thing Shawntel had issues with was being in a relationship with men, which I'm sure half of the world can relate to. She would do anything for her man—I mean anything.

Shawntel met her first love named Jorbin who was a smooth talker, womanizer, charmer, and who was a deacon at the church. He thought every woman wanted him. He was no good for my friend. He would take her for granted because he knew how much she loved him. She would do anything for him. She would give him money, and he would go get pedicures, but he would never ask her to go with him. He was the type of man who would take from a woman. He was arrogant and had more suits than he had drawls. His suits looked hot, outdated, and long. They never fit him right. He would attend church smelling like mothballs and ginger. He swore he was the man. He thought he dressed better than all the men in the church. He would sit in the back of the church and look at all the women who walked by with black shaves on and big earbuds that a customer service rep would wear. You would've thought he was working as a private investigator, a snitch, or a stalker. He was just insane and strange. I would see things that Shawntel couldn't see, but it was not my place to judge or tell her my instincts about him. Jorbin and Shawntel met when they both were twenty-three years old and went to church together. He was everything in a man that Shawntel had ever dreamed of. She had a decent job as a flight attendant, and Jorbin worked offshore. There were time differences with their working schedules; they would plan around their busy schedules to make time for each other. The kids always stayed home with Shawntel's mother, and she would send them to school.

It was in the fall that Shawntel called me and said, "Girl, I love Jorbin but he never tells me how he feels."

"Ok, Shawntel, give the man time, and maybe he'll get around to it. You know men are like turtles. They take their sweet little time but when it comes to being intimate, they move faster than a speeding bullet," I said, laughing.

"I think I want to have another baby, Savannah."

"Shawntel, you can't keep having these babies and throw them off on your mom like she's a day care operator. Look, your mom loves you, but she's getting much older now, and she can't handle running behind kids her entire life. Your mother has a life too! She raised you and your brother as a single mother after your father passed away. Even though you and Jorbin have really good jobs, the kids are being left behind because you both are away all the time and barely spend time with them. You have to be grateful for the ones you have now and be thankful that you have a dedicated and loving mother to help you with the two children you have now."

"You're right, Savannah, that was just wishful thinking!"

"Well, I wish you'd turn off that kind of thinking. You're giving me anxiety," I said, laughing. "Shawntel, just wait patiently and see what happens in the future."

"OK!"

A few weeks passed by, and the economy skyrocketed with the increase of food, utilities, rent mortgages, insurance, education, supplies, and every living expense in the world had been devastating, and it seemed as though nothing would get better. The world was getting extra weird. People wouldn't speak, children skipped school, restaurants were empty because of rising prices, shelters were filling up, and it seemed as though nothing was being done, yet people were still doing the best that they could during all the trials and tribulations. Shawntel called and wanted to meet up at the espresso shop that was one of her favorite hot spots, especially during the winter seasons. We met up, and all of a sudden she said, "I have some good news for you."

I thought she was going to tell me that she was no longer going to be a flight attendant anymore, she was pregnant, or she got a promotion as a leader. She did her job so well, she would deserve it. She quickly held the back side of her left hand up and said, "I'm engaged."

Wow! I was shocked and didn't expect that because Shawntel and I would always have our girly talks before we actually committed to something major.

I gave her a look like, "Really?" I stumbled across my words and said, "Congratulations! Have you set a date yet?"

"No!" she replied.

"I'll be more than happy to help you plan, Shawntel, if you like."

"Ok!" she replied.

Shawntel seemed so full of joy; the sparkles in her eyes were so glistening like she was a shining star.

We live and learn by being educated and experienced. Life can sometimes be like a roller coaster; one day you're up and the next day down. We either relive the past or move forward toward the future. You should never let one bad life lesson hinder you from your blessings. If we didn't fall, we wouldn't be in the position we are in to get back up. There's a season for lessons learned. The blessings that we learned at times seemed as though we could never get a breakthrough. You either swim or you drown. When a tree is planted, it never stops growing. It forms leaves, but even leaves hang on until that season is over, and then new ones grow. That's how life can be. Different seasons for different reasons. If seasons stayed the same, no one would change. Life would be like living in a zombie world.

So it was wedding and planning time. Shawntel and I visited several bridal stores. She was on a budget. The thrift store had a couple of bridal gowns that we visited, but the gowns looked like Carrie from hell. There was only one that was very thrifty that was missing a couple of lace pieces that was on sale for $12.99.

Jokingly, I said, " Here's a bargain for you, Shawntel."

Shawntel giggled and said, "I would not want to be buried in that."

After going from store to store for weeks at a time, she finally found the wedding gown of her dreams. It was a beautiful lace gown with long sleeves and a low-cut neckline; it was modern and longer than what Shawntel wanted. We were so tired and exhausted.

"Shawntel, since you like everything about the gown except that it's extra-long, let's take it to a seamstress."

She agreed! We did just that!

The wedding was months away; there was enough time to have the dress perfected the way she wanted it.

We've decided to go out for drinks. I was a wine and daiquiri girl. Shawntel didn't care. She would drink whatever came her way. I respected her because she knew how to control her drinking and drink responsibly. She was who she was.

After taking several sips of our drinks, we both sat quietly for a minute.

"Shawntel, are you sure you want to marry Jorbin?"

"Yes!" she replied. "I'm sure!"

"Why do you ask, Savannah?"

"Well, I don't know. It's the way he has been treating you."

"Savannah, you know everyone goes through some things with the one they love, and besides Jorbin has gotten a little better. He spends more time with me and the kids. He comes home on the weekends after work, and he's not controlling as much. He takes me and the kids on vacations. We don't argue as much as we used to. We do have disagreements, but we try to make it up before we go to bed. I just wish that Jorbin would change his ways and stop being so flirty with other women. I know that's how he's always been because he was like that with me when we first met. But I don't think he means any harm, and besides he can't be cheating on me if he asked me to marry him."

"Shawntel we've been best friends since elementary, and you know that I would not tell you anything wrong. I'm happy for you. I just wish that you would give it a little bit more time and consideration to really think about it. There's just something about Jorbin that doesn't sit right in my spirit about him."

Shawntel and I did not discuss it any further; we finished our drinks and hors d'oeuvres and hit the dance floor with the rest of the crowd. We joined the line dances and took over. We danced like we never danced before. We owned it like it was ours. It was getting late, and I had to be at work the next day, not knowing what the next day would be like, but of course Shawntel was off for two weeks on vacation from flight attendant duties, so she could have stayed up all night. Her mom had her kids. I don't have kids because I had a hysterectomy many years ago due to cervical cancer, but I must admit I did get pregnant before, but I had a miscarriage. I was stressed out; he was married and had another woman. The girlfriend and his newlywed wife were pregnant at the same time. He confessed, what a loser!

I love kids. I treat Shawntel's kids as if they were my own. They call me Tee-tee Treasure because I always give them money when they do well in school, and believe me they make sure they get on honor roll every semester. I make sure I reward them for every passing grade that they make. They are like my children, and I would do anything for them.

Each day holds a new beginning. You never know what it will be like. I will never forget that a co-worker said to me, "Did you know that when you wake up you have five seconds to plan your day before your brain starts off either negative thinking or planning the day for you?" The next morning I tried it, and it worked. My day was productive, positive thinking. I completed my chores. I treated myself to the spa. I had a facial, pedicure, manicure, full body massage, and of course I had to get a glass of wine. Well to be honest, I had two glasses. I couldn't resist. I was not going to give up free wine, but of course we all know it's included in the price somewhere.

You can't just ignore the problems you are challenged with until you resolve the issues and put them beside you and move forward. That doesn't mean you can't enjoy life in a positive way. You have to squeeze some time in somewhere even if it's in a time-out doing what you love that soothes you like yoga or something more relaxing.

I hadn't heard from Shawntel in over a week. I knew she traveled for a living, so I was sure she would reach out soon. She had been on my mind lately, but of course I worry about the smallest things. I've always been the type of woman to have concerns about people I care about at times. I don't rest or sleep until everyone is safe and accounted for.

My mom used to always tell me I couldn't worry about everything and everybody—that I had to pray and let God handle the rest. I have the best parents in the world. My mom was like me; she told it like it was; she didn't sugarcoat anything. And of course my dad cosigned on whatever Mom said. My mom and I talked just about everything. At a late age, she got sick and had to get a pacemaker and defibrillator. It was a very tough decision for her. Her doctor told her if she didn't, she would have only four years to live. So she did the research and received it. She was a very smart woman. She had more electronics than I did. She knew how to work everything at her age. She would teach me some things. My father would just go with the flow. He loved playing the lottery. Just buy him some lottery tickets, and he was happy and lucky. My parents worked all their lives and retired. We had a good life. Our parents taught us not only to be good at what you did but also be the best at it. And to never ever give up on your dreams, that happiness and peace should always be your priority. My oldest sister was a bully. She used to run behind me with hair, and I would cry and run from it all the time. I was the scared one! My middle sister reminds me of our aunt Darlene. She was the most popular girl in school; she was very brilliant, sassy, and classy. I love and respect my family. I am forever thankful for the bond that we have.

I sent Shawntel several text messages, checked her social media page, and there were no updated posts. That was not like her. She was going to post something, even if it was a silly face. I decided to go by the espresso shop and guess who was there sitting alone? Yes, Shawntel! I ordered my treat and sat by her.

"Hey, are you ok?"

"No," she replied. "Jorbin and I had an argument because he wanted a courthouse wedding. Since this is my very first wedding, I want what every girl dreams of, and that's a big wedding at the church."

"Shawntel, every girl's dream is different, but did you know that you can have the biggest wedding and things still don't work out? Having a justice-of-the-peace wedding might be something you need because, at the rate you two are going, it would not make any sense to have a big wedding and spend all that money and the marriage don't last."

"You just don't want me to have one, Savannah."

"It's not that I don't support you in anything you desire, but what I will not support is being ignorant in denial. You can have whatever you want. It's your life, and you have to live and deal with it, but when the red flags are there, you can't keep putting up green flags and keep going as if you don't see the red flags warning you. It's like you don't just go to the beach and the red flags are flying, and you go dive in the water. You have to take cautions, and if you don't, you could lose your life to something that could have been prevented. You can't build a stable home with an unstable person. Know a bull when you see one. I love you, Shawntel, and I will tell you the truth even if it hurts for you to hear it and understand it. Somebody has to tell the truth. I would rather tell you the truth as a friend than someone in the street tell you differently or not at all. Shawntel, I care about you because if I didn't tell you, you'd look like a fool. I'd rather you spend wisely on something memorable that you would never regret doing and that you could save for something such as going on adventurous, romantic, calm, and soothing trip such as to Hawaii, Dubai, or Los Cabos, Belize, Turks, and Caicos—places you've always wanted to go. You can have a budget wedding and a trip of a lifetime. You'll thank me later!"

I continued, "If you have a big wedding, and the marriage doesn't work, you will be broke, sad, and regret that you never took trips that you'd always wanted to. Shawntel, I'm not in your pocket. I'm trying to save your pocket. It's your life and marriage; I'm just giving you advice. Sometimes a person can see a vision that you don't. I'm not saying that you shouldn't have a wedding because you're right—that's every girl's dream. But if you're not sure and have doubts, then why spend money or waste your time on things you are uncertain of? Anything that's meant to be will be. Never force a person on a horseback ride knowing they can't handle it or aren't securely strapped in. Because it looks easy, it's not always true that anything that's meant to be will never be a debatable discussion."

"Well, Savannah, if it doesn't work out then, it would be on me and not you, and besides it's my wedding."

"Ok, best friend! I respect your decision."

As you can see Shawntel, and I have our opinions and different views, and it's ok to disagree. You have to let one go through it to see the problem and solve it. Life takes us through some hard decisions and journeys. It can either be for the good or the bad. If it's a bad decision, at least you know not to revisit that same road. It's ok to tell people that you love and care about them and their well-being. It makes you a better and concerned friend. If you can't be that honest friend or family member, then what's the sense of having them in your life. A real and genuine friend will tell you the truth. A friend who's not loyal will not tell you the truth; they would rather see you walk the road alone instead of giving you a ride.

It was now time for the bridal shower. Of course I was in charge of the party. It was at a beautiful, nice, and elegant resort. The bridal shower colors were coral and white. The colors were absolutely stunning. The shower consisted of shower favors, games, desserts, the cocktail bar, a food bar of Italian, African, and American foods, which were Shawntel's favorites, and of course the sweetest sugars of everything you could imagine. The cake was a typical standout cake, coral and white swirl inside and out with coral-colored cream cheese frosting. The bar was decorated with assorted cocktails and chardonnay, sauvignon blanc, and pinot grigio wines to choose from, surrounding beautiful flowers and greenery plants. The bridesmaids brought early gifts. The DJ played some smooth soul jazz music. There were no strippers at the bridal shower. I wanted Shawntel to be relaxed and full of love, joy, and happiness and have herself the most memorable time of her life. It was all about her.

The bridal shower lasted for about five hours. Everyone was tired, so we all called it a night because tomorrow was the wedding day. I know it might seem strange as to why we had the bridal shower the day before the wedding. Again it was all about Shawntel, and that's what she wanted. I had to grant her wishes. I was glad to kill two birds with one stone all within hours of each other. I was getting tired, and I was ready for all of it to be over. It had driven me insane. We all had a few drinks. We did not indulge because we knew we had to be right and focused for the wedding tomorrow. I didn't get to bed until around 3:00 a.m. I cleaned up and finished eating the lobster and shrimp dip and seafood lasagna, which I had hidden in the fridge from the girls. They would have eaten it all up and not focused on other dishes that were provided. And you know damn well I was not about to waste food and my money. They were going to eat hot dogs and chips, but of course there were other cultural foods they really enjoyed. I was not going to bore them out like that. Tomorrow was a big day, and I needed to get some rest because I didn't know what it was going to bring. I was just wishing all the best for my girl Shawntel and Jorbin. I hoped what they were going through was just a relief that was needed in order for both of them to move forward to their new journey and life together. It was normal to be nervous and curious if you had any questions and concerns that bothered you. It was best to get all the anger and doubts out and discuss any and all concerns that you may have with each other. Going into a marriage with a clear and concise, focused, good spirit and a genuine heart is what makes part of the marriage intriguing and engaging.

In just a few hours Shawntel would be Mrs. Jorbin Slater. She was nervous, and I was nervous for her.

Everyone had their hair done alike, manicures and pedicures were done, gowns and heels were on feet. The makeup artist was running late, and Shawntel was freaking out.

"Calm down—maybe she's stuck in traffic or something."

"No, Savannah! It is unacceptable! I paid her a deposit to be on time and do the job."

"I understand Shawntel!" At this point Shawntel was all moody and was not trying to hear it. She was going to sweat her hair out if she kept it up.

"Just be patient. She's coming, and besides if the makeup artist doesn't show up, I know how to do makeup."

"Oh Lord," Shawntel giggled and shook her head.

"They may not like themselves, but I will do my best."

As soon as I said that, the makeup artist showed up and was two hours late. Shawntel was ticked off! We were all trying to calm her down.

Shawntel was furious. "Let me go! I'm ok I just need a moment to snap back." She went into the bathroom, took off her wedding dress, wrapped her hair up in a hairnet and hair bonnet, and came back out with some tennis shoes and shorts on and some Vaseline. She immediately snatched Katie the make-up artist's ponytail out, and that was it. We looked at Shawntel, and we were like, "You took off your wedding dress, put on some street clothes just to snatch out a ponytail? Jesus take the wheel!"

Finally the wedding was over and the wedding reception went very well. Jorbin and Shawntel both looked absolutely in love and stunning. It was a very long and interesting day. Everyone on the guest list showed up, and the food and beverages were on point. All I could say was I would never ever in life plan another wedding again. Just let me sit at the bar and get drunk girl wasted.

Shawntel and Jorbin's marriage was going well for about four years. I didn't hear much from Shawntel. When she was able to go out on a girl's outing, we would make up for missed times. But on this one particular day the sun was out, the skies were blue, it was breezy, and I'd noticed she would text me more and more especially in the wee hours of the night. I knew something wasn't right.

She reached out to me and said, "Savannah, Jorbin and I have been arguing and fighting over nonsense."

"What do you mean, Shawntel? What's going on?"

"Well, I don't know! He barely comes home on the weekends, and when he does, he's in and he's out. He says he's hanging out with friends, shooting pool, and having a drink or two. I understand he deserves to spend time with his friends but seemingly too often. I had a talk with Jorbin, and he said there was nothing wrong with leaving his offshore job and accepting another job in South Carolina that pays well. I asked Jorbin why he didn't discuss anything with me. He said why should he—that he's the king and whatever decisions he makes, it's his business and not mine. That was a big slap in the face to me."

"Wow! I am sorry to hear that."

"It's ok, Savannah. It will get better. I'm just hoping all of this is because maybe he's stressed out at work and wanting more for us since he and I've been married."

"Maybe you and Jorbin should seek counseling. I have a really good pastor that you both can sit down and talk with. I'm sure he doesn't mind. My pastor has prayed for me in some difficult situations."

Marriages can fail due to lack of communication, not supporting or respecting one's decision, and or failing to accept or own up to wrongdoings. Marriage is something you cannot bring friends and family into who you can't trust or who or not willing to help the both of you fix the problem. Marriage is not for everyone, but separation and divorces are preventable. When you're both in love but have very small problems and are willing to make it work, then it's easy patching up smaller problems. You can't build and force a home when the foundation is not stable. It's ok to let go, but you have to make sure that's what you both want to do. But don't rush into another relationship without closing the door on the other one, or you'll only have bigger problems than the one you already have. Respecting yourself and healing is the most important step to moving forward.

I decided to reach out to Shawntel to see how she was doing. Of course her husband was at home, so she really could not talk that long, but during the conversation I could hear Jorbin yelling at her.

"Shawntel, are you ok? I can call you back another time."

"Oh no, Savannah! I'm fine! He's upset because he thinks I'm telling you all of our business. He's just having a moment. You know, Savannah, we're going to take your advice and go to counseling, and also I'd love to meet up with your pastor for prayer. Jorbin said he'd go this time."

Surprisingly he agreed to go, only to please Shawntel. I hoped that whatever the pastor could do could save the marriage. Shawntel would be so pleased.

Jorbin finally settled into his new apartment in South Carolina, and Shawntel remained at her home in Florida. Somehow it seemed to work for the both of them for a little while until Jorbin seemed to be working more, but his paychecks never mounted up to the hours he claimed to have worked. Shawntel's job was cutting hours, and she was barely making ends meet. She asked Jorbin why he was slacking on making deposits into their family account that she needed for bills, food, the children's clothing, healthcare, etc. Jorbin's excuse was they cheated him out of his pay. He had been saying that for months. One day Shawntel was curious as to why Jorbin always made excuses as to why he never answered the phone or told her to call before she took a flight to South Carolina. As his wife she shouldn't have had to call him beforehand. She was better than me. I'd pop up like a jack-in-the-box on him. See, Shawntel and I are definitely two different people. The things that Jorbin did and said to her would be zero tolerance for me. I'd have rung his neck like a wet washcloth and slung his turkey-neck self on the laundry line with clothespins stuck all up his butt and left him out there for days hoping it got hotter than Cayenne Carolina Reaper pepper mixed with 106-degree weather. One thing was for certain and two things for sure, if Jorbin was my husband, I'd have had him in a time-out corner somewhere milking a cow. I told Shawntel a few years back that if she didn't stop and recognize the game, she would always get played. You have to be in charge of your controller, or you will lose every time.

Winter was finally here, and yes, Shawntel was still going at it with Jorbin. She decided to catch a flight and go visit him unexpectedly. She wanted to surprise him.

Her flight landed, and she called to let me know that she had made it to South Carolina.

"Ok, be safe, and I pray you and Jorbin can work things out and try to be a little bit more peaceful and understanding with each other," I said.

"Savannah, how much peace and understanding do I need when he's done a lot of terrible things to me verbally and physically?"

"Physically? What do you mean by physically, Shawntel? Did he put his hands on you?"

"Savannah, we will finish this conversation later. I have to go now. Love you!"

Shawntel had a key to his apartment. When he drove to Georgia to see her and the children, he took melatonin because he has insomnia and needed to get some rest. He was severely tired and exhausted. Shawntel took his keys while he was asleep, went to the key shop, and made a copy of his key while he slept away. She made her way inside the apartment. It was nicely decorated with a woman's touch because Jorbin would never! He didn't even know how to unclog a toilet. Now Jorbin was not a decorator; he was too impatient for that. She took a walk throughout the entire apartment, opened the refrigerator, and there were bottles of assorted wines. She was so excited because he knew how she liked wine, and he had stashes of wine stored on the bar as well as a couple of bottles in the refrigerator. She walked through the apartment, smiling because she was really proud of how Jorbin kept the apartment really elegant.

She then reached the bathroom and saw hair products, which could be used for a man or a woman.

Since she hadn't seen Jorbin for a few weeks, she thought maybe he wanted to change. He wore his hair in a tapered type of haircut, where the sides were trimmed with hair on top, more of an elaborate pompadour style. He kept his face neat in appearance, with no beard but with a light mustache. He always was a well-dressed man. Chile, you would have thought he had landed a magazine deal. She continued to tour the apartment and went into his bedroom; she snooped into every area of the room. Shawntel was feeling kind of at ease that she didn't find enough evidence to convict him with. She thought she was just overreacting. She trusted Jorbin and believed that their marriage could be saved. Well, let's just say until she dug a little bit deeper.

Around 11:00 p.m. Shawntel called Jorbin asking where he was? He said he was at work. She decided to cook dinner, light candles, and have the apartment smelling aromatic and looking romantic. She ran warm bathwater and added some Moroccan scented foaming bubble bath with rose petals in the tub and aligned rose petals from the entry door leading to the bathroom. She cooked Jorbin's favorite meal, lobster alfredo with dinner rolls and lemon water to drink. Why he drank lemon water with the fancy meal, I don't know, but whatever rocked his boat let him float. She knew him better!

Just when she thought everything was all peaches and cream just by adding a little cherry on top, it got very interesting.

Shawntel was in the room and putting on her lingerie. She always wore it for him after she showered, with some smooth jazz playing in the background and a glass of chardonnay. She heard a clicking sound of the key as if Jorbin was getting ready to enter, and she got very excited. She was glowing, smelling refreshed. Her hair was a short bob style cut, she had a French manicure, her body was oiled down, and she was glistening, standing there with a smile. Her heart was pounding. She was nervous because at this point she was not sure if this would make or break the marriage.

The door opened and Shawntel's eyes widened and her mouth dropped. It was a woman walking through the door. The unknown woman at the time dropped her keys and dinner she had brought for her and Jorbin.

She asked, "Who are you and why are you in my apartment?"

Shawntel replied, "Your apartment? Jorbin is my husband and why are you here?"

"I'm here because this is my and Jorbin's apartment and has been for three years and counting, sweetheart. And by the way, my name is Noretta. Nice to meet you too! Look lady, I don't know who you are and why you are still standing in my house. I suggest you get out before I call the police."

"Well, call them because I'm not leaving without my husband."

"You can stay and sleep in the doghouse right beside Fluffy eating some Kibbles 'N Bits because you're sure not staying in my house with Jorbin and me."

Shawntel and Noretta both begin texting Jorbin out of control. Jorbin never answered the calls or returned any of the texts. Where Jorbin worked there was a lot of noise, so of course he was not going to hear the phone as he always said. Besides he kept it on vibrate. Shawntel would get onto Jorbin for that because it could be an emergency situation regarding the children. But he never listened to her. After all the commotion, Noretta finally showed the apartment lease to Shawntel with Jorbin's name on it.

Shawntel immediately called me upset and cried out of control, explaining what happened. I listened to her and felt really sorry about the situation. I had said something many times that there was something about Jorbin that I did not like. She was my friend, and I had to listen and comfort her the best way I knew how. She was out of money, and I had to send her money to pay for a flight back home.

"Why would you pay for a one-way flight?"

"Because Jorbin would have paid for me to get back, and I'm his wife, and I'm sure he didn't mind."

"Married or not, you should never depend on or put all your trust and financial situations as a person's responsibility, and you know how wishy-washy Jorbin is."

"Savannah, enough of your speech! Are you going to send me the money or not?"

"Not until you ask me with a better attitude than that."

"Bossy lady, will you send me some money, please ma'am, so that I can come home to my kids?"

"Sure I will. I will do anything for you!"

"Oooh! you get on my nerves, Savannah!"

"I love you too, Shawntel!"

"Please do not tell my mom about any of this ok, Savannah?"

"Okey dokey!"

She finally made it back home, and Jorbin had yet to reach back out from the previous calls and texts. I was sure the drama would come up with some lame excuses as usual.

From sunrise to sunset you never know what each day will be. You can start off a good day and end up with a bad day. It depends on how you start your day off—whether you spend it alone or doing other activities that keep you focused and productive, such as spending time with friends and family. Splurge a little bit and pamper yourself. You can avoid drama if you don't put yourself around it, but that's not always the case. Sometimes drama can find you. It's up to you to engage in it or not.

Shawntel's problem was that she had to learn to move in silence; everything didn't need a reaction. The best reaction is to react in an adult manner and mind your business. She was once that way, but once she married Jorbin, it was like she stopped at a yield sign, got confused, and didn't know which way to go.

Now the drama kept going and going like a nev-er-ending circus. She finally heard from Jorbin, and she confronted him. "Jorbin, I know you received my text messages, calls, and voice messages. Why am I just hearing from you?"

Jorbin replied, "Baby, you know I've told you before, I work in the plant, and there's so much noise that there's barely any signal in the building. I'm sure a lot of the voice messages are spam calls anyway. But I love you, baby. How are you and the kids doing?"

"The kids are fine, and I love you too! I finally talked to my boss, and now that there are funds in the budget, he decided to give the employees a raise and bonuses. I can talk to my boss about anything and he listens. Why can't you be like that, Jorbin?"

"Because I am me, and he is he!"

Shawntel replied, "You're such a smarty pants. Jorbin, honey, how was your week, and how are you liking the new job? I know it's all the beginning process, and you're not used to being around crowds. You can be antisocial at times."

"It's ok, baby. Once I get used to the job and the people, I think I'll be able to manage. I guess it takes time. Look, babe, I have to go now, I will call you later tonight before you fall asleep. I love you and the kids."

"We love you too, honey."

Wasn't that strange? Jorbin hadn't mention anything about Shawntel being in his apartment or anything about her. He thought Shawntel didn't know about any of this, but she thought that maybe he was tired—who knew.

If Jorbin was not going to say anything then she would not either. She would do anything to keep him calm and at peace. She would do anything for her man.

Now that Shawntel thought Jorbin was still as good as golden because he never mentioned a thing about the mistress he lived with, she thought she could carry on like nothing ever happened. She was good. There was no way I could have kept my mouth closed in a situation like that; I was too outspoken, and there was no man that golden to make me forget about what happened. I'd bring up the past, present, and the future. I guess this is why we are all born with our own minds, hearts, and the way we feel about people, places, and things. If we all thought the same way, can you imagine how much and what we all would be missing that could be a blessing or a lesson to us?

On Saturday morning Shawntel and I of course went to the expresso coffee shop where we had our usual and a good old thick, old-fashioned chocolate brownie, knowing this should be the last thing on our minds. Too many calories, but you only live once, so why not indulge.

At the moment it was not about Shawntel. The conversation was about me and my past experiences with relationships. Shawntel was always open with me, and I was never open with her like I should because I've always been a private woman. And Shawntel told Jorbin our business when he asked her because he was too busy making sure I was not setting her up with anyone. He said weird things all the time out of the norm. He was just weird like that. Not everything, but some things she'd tell him, and it was ok as long as she knew her limit. I didn't mind, but she needed to focus on what and who she was in a relationship with. I'd always kept it short, sweet, and simple.

"Savannah, get out those little girl panties and put on some real big girl panties," Shawntel said with a laugh. "You know the ones that fit you and grip?!"

Shawntel could be funny at times, but I loved her with all that I have within me.

We began to sip on our lattes and eat some pepper jack cheese and ham slices and watched other customers pass by and enjoy each other. We decided to take a little walk in the area and talk.

"So, Savannah, how's it going with you?"

"It's going great! I definitely wouldn't put up with what you're going through. I'll get rid of a man real quick. I don't stick around. Well, girl, for starters, best friend, I was dating this guy named Mathias. Let's just say Mathias had it going on. He was so fine. He was designed and built just the way I wanted in a man. It was as though the Lord knew how I liked my men. He was very pleasant and polite. He would open the car doors for me, take me out to dinner, and pay all of my bills. And did I mention that he definitely won the best romance man award of the year? I was ready for that man that same night. His kisses and touches were so amazing. He was always generous, respectful, loving, and kind. And believed in communication. He took great care of me. Even though we didn't live in the same state, he would always reach out to me no matter what time of the day or the hour. It was very important to me. He was not an everyday drinker but a social drinker. The best part that blew me away was that he was definitely in love with wine. Now you know he won me over. He did not discriminate at all. Whatever I wanted to drink, honey, he was game for it. He would go to social events with me, comedy shows, and line dances. He was everything to me and then some. He was a man who could not be duplicated.

"Months went by, so we decided to get serious. This monster had a whole wife and two other girlfriends. How did I find out? Mathias went to the restroom and left his cell phone on the breakfast bar, and of course you know me—I snooped to see who was calling. Redbone called six times. The phone rang, and it was a girl named Funds. What kind of name is that? My guess is maybe she's a fool to give him money. She called twice, and then there was a call from a wife named Carla. I read a few of his text messages where all three women were pregnant at the same time. The wife and Redbone were due three weeks apart. Oh my goodness! At this point I was speechless and confused.

"Mathias finally came out of the bathroom. I didn't say anything. It was none of my business, but it was in the beginning for me to be snooping in his messages, and besides we were never in a serious relationship anyway. He made me feel like the queen I'd never experienced before. I just dealt with him because I was bored, and I had nothing else better to do. He was not loyal at all. I could not resist the temptation, which is not good at all knowing what kind of man he was.

"With everything that I was going through, this would not stop me from dating ever again. There's a season and a reason for everything. I'm not willing to be anyone's doormat. I've told myself many times that I would not be used by anyone. My time is valuable; my worth is golden. My standards are high, and my worth is knowing that I deserve more than just settling for anything and for less than. When you settle for anything, you get less than what you deserve."

It was a new day and a new beginning. I invited Shawntel to come over and have a pool party. I decided to break out the master grill and cook steaks, chicken, and shrimp, rainbow pasta salad, asparagus, summer whole kernel, and of course the martinis. But before I grilled, we decided to set the timer on who could swim the fastest. I was moving in slow motion, slower than a snail, a turtle, and a worm. I'm not a good swimmer. Shawntel can swim. Well at least she thinks she can swim, but really she swims slower than me. Neither one of us won! We both were tired after the first stroke. As we got out of the pool to sit in the lounge chairs, we went to make martinis. We relaxed a little while sipping on martinis, listened to some smooth jazz, and relaxed. It was a beautiful day. We couldn't let the day go by without enjoying the day that the creator had created. What a good day it was.

"Savannah, I'm so thankful for our friendship no matter what I've been through," Shawntel said. "You've always been there for me. Even though we may have disagreements at times, you've never walked away from our friendship. I don't think I could ever repay you as much as you have done for me."

"Awe! You're welcome. That's what friends are for. We do have our ups and downs, but you're smart and mentoring yourself. You've done so much for me and I thank you for that. Remember that time you were getting child support from Jorbin, and you said, 'Jorbin is a good father' because at the time he was paying you child support, and you let him claim the kids on your taxes?"

"Yes! I remember that, Savannah!"

"And then I said, 'Shawntel, what are you thinking? He's getting his child support that he pays you back by claiming the kids on his taxes every year.' And you looked at me like a deer looking at bright headlights."

"He was so angry with me, Savannah. He didn't speak to me for months. If it was not about our children, he didn't want anything to do with me. He was stubborn and wanted things his way. His father was like that, and I guess like father like son. His mom was very down-to-earth. Even though I believe she didn't care for me as much because I took her son from her. He was a momma's boy. She didn't have too much control over him. He had to choose where he would eat dinner—at our home or spend Christmas and Thanksgiving with his mom. It was always some drama between his mom and I, but we got over it and moved on."

Shawntel can sometimes take feelings the wrong way. If she took the time to rekindle the relationship she had with Jorbin's mother, maybe they both could have gotten to know each other better. One small misunderstanding can leave you in a situation of longevity of miscommunication and pain. Jorbin didn't seem to care. He sparked the situation by not sitting both Shawntel or his mother down to have a conversation with the both of them. I think taking time out for the both of them to settle their differences would be a relief of stress to settle their differences. It was something that could be fixed. It would have been good for the kids. They were in the middle and saw the unselfish behavior of all parties. No one was thinking about the children, who needed the most attention. The children woke up in the middle of the night crying, which was affecting their physical and mental health. The children were not active, and I was sure it had a lot to do with the situation.

"But Savannah, I want the perfect life, the perfect husband, and the perfect family."

"Shawntel, you can't have the perfect life if you're trying to build a foundation that's not leveled and strong enough to hold it in place. There is no perfect life, only in a dream, and even dreams aren't real."

"What do you know about life, Savannah?"

"I've been there; that's why I'm trying to save you. You don't have to travel the same road. You have to select a different path, and you'll find a new road to happiness."

Shawntel did not listen to one thing that I said to encourage her.

The next day Jorbin called Shawntel and asked her for a divorce. She became furious, sad, depressed, and a couch potato. She quit her job and lost her house and car. She stopped going to parent and teacher meetings when the children were failing in school. She lost her faith, she quit going to church, praying, and meditating. Her hair and appearance was never kept up. She walked around like she was lost. Her house was always dark with blackout curtains. There was no internet or cable. She lost interest in what she loved, knitting and gardening.

I stopped by to see if Shawntel wanted to go to her favorite espresso shop to sit and drink our favorites. Surprisingly she declined to go.

"Get out your feelings," I said. "It's not the end of the world. You must get out of the mood you're in. People have relationship problems every day. You're not in this alone. You have me, your mom, your pastor, other leaders, and your children, who want nothing but the best for you. I'm sure if you discuss

your situation with your mom she would understand; she should be your number one person to be
confided in. She's your backbone even more than I
am. I understand what you are going through, and
it is not easy, but you can't sit around feeling sorry
for yourself. You have a beautiful soul and family
to think about. Relationships come and go. You've
lost so much weight, and it is not healthy. You have
your entire life ahead of you, and it is not too late to
regain it back respectfully."

"Savannah, there's something I need to tell you."

"What is it?"

"I've been fighting a neurological disorder where my
face and body aches all the time. My face constantly
hurts when I eat, laugh, talk, and even when I comb
my hair. I've been diagnosed with this for almost
a year now. I'm currently fighting neuralgia disorder. I'm fighting dysarthria and anarthria. It affects
my speech among other things. I've been fighting
this alone, and this is why I've been fighting for my
marriage. I'm sure if I told Jorbin, he wouldn't see
the beauty in me anymore. He would look at me

like I was nobody, and it will hurt me to the core of my soul. I haven't told my mom; she's already going through enough. She keeps my kids, battling with diabetes, cancer, high blood pressure, and so much more. I don't want to put too much on her right now than she can handle."

"Oh, best friend! I'm so sorry! Anything you need, I'm here for you. Just be honest and open, and we can get through this together. I will not judge you, but you have to be tough for your children and have enough strength to fight back. You can do this. You got this! We got this! Together we can get through anything if we just trust and believe. Are you telling your mom and Jorbin about your situation?"

"When the time is right, Savannah."

"Now is the time. "You can get the support and help that you need but only you can want and desire for it. But I respect your timing."

Being patient with Shawntel was something that she needed right then. She was going through hell and back, and Jorbin wasn't making it any better. He was not supportive enough. He had no compassion and understanding of what he was putting his wife through. He didn't take the time to spend with her. All he cared about was what he could do and get from the next. He had always been a lowlife of a father figure and a boyfriend. He disrespected and controlled his mother, belittled her as if she was a nobody. If he had grown up in my neighborhood back in the day and disrespected a woman, he'd be a better person than he is today.

Shawntel begged Jorbin not to divorce her and said that they could work through anything. He told her he was in love with another woman.

She finally confronted Jorbin that she knew all about the woman he was seeing. Of course, as Jorbin said, "You don't need to tell me. I've seen you at my apartment. There's cameras all around my apartment. I saw you when you came in, snooped through my things. While I was asleep you took my house key and made a copy. I have a smart key; it alerted me that a duplicate key was made to my apartment, the location it was done at, and the time."

Jorbin had been treating Shawntel and the kids like they were not his family. He didn't take them anywhere or call the kids like he should have. He was just a mess! He could tell her anything and she would believe it. One time he gave her a watch. He told her he had had it for quite some time but wanted to give it to her. He did not give it to her at the time because of how she had been treating him, which was a lie. He had that for a woman who he was cheating with. However, the relationship had failed when he found out that the other woman was still married. I kind of knew the woman he was cheating with and so did Shawntel. We were on the dance team many, many years ago called, "Just A Girl's Dream." Jorbin was a habitual liar. He was an industrious liar. His deceitfulness would make you believe everything he said. He told a lie so well with a straight face. He was a womanizer. He claimed to be in church as a deacon, that he was more dedicated than ever before.

Yeah right!

Jorbin picked Shawntel and the kids up in the church van. She had lost everything, including her car. I just hoped she could get to see how Jorbin really was one day. He slept with everyone in the church. She really thought he loved her. He was a man who loved attention and compliments. He thought I was always in the way. I was a genuine friend, and he knew that. He would always bring women into their home while Shawntel was working. He confessed to her only because the next door neighbor had an outdoor camera and showed Shawntel the trafficking. Yet she remained with him.

One day Shawntel and I were on the way to the store, and her daughter was saying, "Momma, Daddy had a lady at the house." She ignored what her daughter was trying to tell her, that Daddy was kissing another girl. She would always tell the kids to go sit down and play with the toys. I don't know if she knew what was going on all that time, was in denial, or just did not care.

On a Wednesday morning Shawntel reached out to me and wanted to have lunch. At that moment I knew my friend was going through something, and she wanted to talk.

"I said, sure! What about 10:30 a.m.?"

"Ok! Sounds like a plan!"

We met at a small cafe that we'd never been to before and decided to try it. If we didn't like it, we would never visit that again.

We finally made it to the hole-in-the-wall, and I asked, "Are you sure we want to meet here?"

Shawntel replied, "Girl, now you know these holes-in-the-wall have the best foods, and besides I looked at the reviews, and it rated four stars."

At that moment I knew we were going to leave with satisfaction. Shawntel ordered soup and a salad. I looked at her and said, "What in the heck is that? You should have stayed at home to eat that." However, I had an appetite. I ordered rib eye steak, asparagus, red potatoes, and not one glass of wine, but two.

"Savannah, I have been going through so much. Since my husband doesn't want me anymore, I guess I'll have to find a new man. I do have one in mind. Savannah, do you remember that handsome, 6' 2",

152-pound, bald, well-dressed, nice body, smart, handsome, and very intelligent man who worked at the law firm of Leaves and Somerville? His name is Chase. I used to date him a year before I met Jorbin."

"Oh, yes! I remember him."

"We were young. We grew apart, went to college, and never reconnected. He reached out to me on social media. He's very successful. He now has his own law firm and is doing well. He owns four properties and lives in San Diego, California. He was married and is now a widow with two children. His wife passed away from injuries from a car accident as she was leaving from a women's conference down in Miami, Florida. Chase still hasn't completely healed from his loss but is maintaining staying strong and focused for his children. He was always good to me. But at the time I had just met Jorbin, and I wanted to find love again. And at that time Jorbin was the one."

"Shawntel, you have to close your doors before opening up to others. Don't be that woman who holds on to something that no longer serves you. I mean maybe you can try counseling or seeing your pastor for consultation. That's a start at least for the sake of your kids and the effort. I can get the kids, and you and Jorbin can go out for a nice evening, and you can talk about it."

"Thank you, Savannah, for your advice. Jorbin doesn't want to do any of that. He thinks he can resolve every situation on his own. Which would make the situation worse. I really want to date Chase and see where the relationship can take us."

"I support your decision-making as long as you're happy and make the right decisions for you and especially for those kids of yours. It's not about just the mom or the dad being happy; it's the kids as well because it will affect their lives on a daily basis. I hope he's a praying man and knows the Lord. The man I dated before named Jonathan once told me to never pray for him again because my prayers weren't sincere enough. He was a deacon in the church that would be in every woman's social media pages and in their messengers. But of course evidently my prayers worked. He lived to tell the testimony of his health status. His other prayer warriors who he put before me had left him and stopped praying when they thought he was better. I stayed in prayer for him before, during, and afterward. I did what God wanted me to do. I have a caring heart and I would never let anyone question my faith or what I believe in. At the end of the day, I would never regret what I have done that is in the favor of God. When we pray for others, our personal levels connect with God. A man who doesn't trust and believe in God and mistreats others does not have a personal relationship with God, in my opinion. A man who tries to lead his own life on his own because he thinks he's the king and knows self-destruction and low self-esteem will have a difficult time listening to others and a hard time in life. Man cannot lean into his own understanding without knowing and following God's purpose and plans—that I believe. It just doesn't always work that way. You will only reap what you sow."

"Oh! There you go, Savannah, with your speeches," Shawntel said, laughing. "You definitely are telling the truth. You know that I love you through it all."

"I just keep it real. You know I love you too best friend, and there's nothing in the world that I would not do for you, Shawntel. I just want you to protect your heart. Even though we are adults, we're never too old to speak the truth. It's all about learning, understanding, and accepting the truth and growth."

"Savannah, I just feel so embarrassed going through what I'm going through and putting you all through this and giving you my problems. I isolate and feel alone at times."

"Shawntel, I've been through so much, but I'm not embarrassed about anything I've been through. It's all a lesson but at the same time it turned out to be a blessing. What's gossip for others turns out to be a blessing for me. I have invited people to my table and shared some of my blessings with them. All the pieces they thought were broken were fixed and healed by having faith, believing and trusting in the Lord. I can go on and on. By the way, my steak and asparagus is getting cold, and you know I'm not going to tell the waiter to put my plate in the microwave to reheat. Well if I tip him well enough he just might."

"Savannah, I don't want this salad anymore. You talked me to death. That worked up an appetite.

Give me a piece of that steak and two of those asparagus, girl," Shawntel said with a chuckle.

After we finished our conversation and ate brunch, I began to think that Shawntel was just going through menopause with hot flashes or a phase and just needed to cool off and get it together. You have to be grateful for that to do better, be better, and to know better. I believe that God separates us from the good and the bad. He gives us seasons and reasons, lessons and blessings, to learn to plant the seed and water to see our harvest to grow. One should never feel alone or regret anything that failed. Failing is just the start to finish. Trust the process, believe it, and you shall receive it.

I'd always thought Jorbin was weird. He wasn't weird; he just showed who he really was, and he was tired of hiding and faking it. He couldn't keep a straight face for too long. I thought he really loved Shawntel, but his love didn't change overnight.

The more I thought about Shawntel and Jorbin's relationship, the more I realized there was a lack of communication between the both of them. I tried not to get into their business, but being Shawntel's best friend, I would always be there for her no matter what. That's what loyal friends are for. Of course she had her mom, but I thought she was more comfortable talking to me on a personal level.

They should have been more open with her mom. I just hoped it wasn't too late that she regretted not telling her mom everything that she was dealing with.

Sometimes in life we don't quite understand everything when it comes to relationships, yet we try to force the pieces of the puzzle together, ask questions with no clear or conscious answer, and still don't understand it all. You have to find your peace and a perfect relaxation place to clear your mind and spirit.

Jorbin was still on the prowl, looking for who knew what. He had everything he needed at home: a beautiful wife who loved him unconditionally and two beautiful children who were innocent to all of this. Jorbin wanted nothing to do with me because he thought I was controlling Shawntel's life. If anything he was ruining her life.

He sent me a message over social media saying that he knew that his wife and I had been best friends for years, but he just thought I should mind my own business.

Before I knew it, I told him to grow some balls because he was probably not big enough to handle and stop the bowling pins from falling over. After I said that, Jorbin did not write back.

A guilty person is always in defense mode. Jorbin just assumed without investigating the situation. I reached out to Shawntel to let her know that Jorbin had reached out to me with that mess.

"Savannah, don't worry about that. He's still doing the same thing—lying and cheating." And Shawntel asked Jorbin for a divorce. "I'm just waiting for this to be over with. I'm going to let him do him. He will see once I'm gone and out of his life what a beautiful and gorgeous wife he had with his beautiful children. He will reap what he sowed!"

"Shawntel, I support you, and I am here for you every step of the way no matter what. Anything you need, I got you."

"Since you're in the offering mood, the kids and I need a place to stay until I get on my feet."

"Yes! You and the kids can come here with me as long as you want to. Just make sure the kids of yours don't eat up all my butter pecan ice cream."

"Oh hush, Savannah! You better be worried because that's my favorite too!" she said, laughing.

"All right! You and your children are going to be sleeping in the doghouse with Flipper and her babies," I said, laughing.

"I filed for a divorce on his birthday! A day he will never forget."

"Wow, Shawntel, I didn't think you had it in you. I support you, and I respect your decision as long as you both play a big part in the kids' lives."

"Well, if he doesn't then he will never see his kids again."

"Don't take the kids away, Shawntel. They didn't do anything. They are innocent. All they need right now is love, guidance, and support from both parents."

"You're right, Savannah. You've always been a peace-maker. In your afterlife you should come back as a puzzle, you're always putting things together," Shawntel said, chuckling.

"Oh hush, Shawntel," I said, chuckling.

Going through a divorce or ending a relationship can be alarming and devastating especially if you have children involved and you thought your marriage would last forever. It can! It takes sacrificing, love, and communication to make it work both ways, and both must be willing to go to the extreme to build that trust and not engage in destructive behavior.

Shawntel was furious that Jorbin had a lawyer.

How in the world could he afford a lawyer?

"Savannah, I don't know how that's possible unless he had been hiding money from me all this time, saving up. I'm going to lose this because he will try to get custody of our children. He has no time for them either. I wish I had a lawyer. I can't afford one, and I can barely feed myself and my children. I'm doing the best that I can. This is so hard for me," Shawntel cried.

"Relax, Shawntel! I know this is a lot to take in, but if you have faith and trust in the Lord, Jorbin can't stand a chance in court. Besides what man wants the custody of their children if they're barely making it themselves?"

"I don't know, Savannah. Maybe an evil person who does not care about hurting others. I never thought he would do this to me."

Divorce court was the next Wednesday, and Shawntel was ready. I pulled up to her apartment, she walked out, and she looked fabulous. She was relaxed, motivated, and positively stunning, and she was dressed from head to toe. She had on her two-piece white suit, her hair was slayed, and with her Chanel jewelry on, she was on point. This girl was on fire. As she stepped out of the car, she said, "I am my own lawyer, and I got this."

"Ok, slay bae. You got this girl. Good luck, bestie!"

A few hours passed by, and I had not heard anything from her. My thoughts were all over the place. I thought maybe there had been a delay for the court hearing or something, but if I knew Shawntel like I knew her, she was going to call. And sure thing moments later, the phone rang, and it was slay bae.

I answered, "Hello, slay bae," I giggled. "How did it go?"

"I agreed to share parenting. He has to pay child support and alimony until I get a job, and the judge ordered me to get a job within eighteen months. Jorbin will be responsible for all day care, medical, healthcare, and dental expenses. That was one of the most expensive bills ever. He thought he was doing the thing. All he did was create more responsibilities for himself, which he should have been doing anyway. I'm keeping his last name. Just like Tina Turner said, "I work too damn hard for it to give it up," Shawntel laughed. "And the mistress who he was cheating on me with paid for all of his legal fees. And they're supposed to be getting married. He's only marrying her because she has money. And he's sorry and don't want to do anything, but now he has to really work.

"I hope they do get married so she can pay his extra bills, the alimony for him. It doesn't matter who pays it as long as it gets paid accurately and timely. It's on court records and needs to be paid to me in a timely manner. Thank you, Lord!"

"Now that that's behind you, you can now focus on you and the kids more, and because your divorce is legal, don't be all wild and out and give away your polly cake," I laughed. "Take some time out for yourself. Relationships come and go, but mental and emotional health can stay with you if you don't take care of yourself," I said. "Let's set a date and time so we can tell your mom what's really been going on in your life. If you're scared I can go with you, but being an adult, I think you should go alone, privately."

"Ok! I think I'll go alone and talk to mom," Shawntel said.

The hardest part of divorce is taking that step to actually filing it. Life can sometimes be unfair, and we must take whatever comes at us and deal with it the best way we know how. Everything good is not always bad, and everything bad is not always good. Each day has its own challenges. There are pastors and counselors who we can seek, but sometimes that's not enough to change the thoughts and how we react to everything. We have to be careful to think before reacting. Once you get through the hurdles and the stumbling blocks, it gets easier to think and make decisions of the best interests that meet both needs. You can't win a game and lose every time, but one thing you can do is be the solution and not the problem. Divorces don't mean to take everything from each other. If you're a reconciling and forgiving person, one should do the right thing, and that's divide equally.

Shawntel's new beginning had started, and she was already healing, looking fabulous, motivated and ready to start over. She was no longer a flight attendant; she wanted to spend more time at home with her children. She worked at home with a multimillion dollar company in the makeup, arts, and fashion industry. She had her own website, and business for her was going well. She and her mom had progressed. She had been more open and honest with her mom as she should have, and I was so proud of her.

We still had our girls outings at the expresso cafe. In fact I would be meeting her in a few hours to catch up on some things and move forward from the past. But of course we would revisit the past from time to time. Some things just were not that easy to get over. It was all a part of the healing process, of memories that our brain holds on to so that we could be reminded to not go down that road again or make bad decisions. This how we get to the present of our new beginnings.

We met up at our favorite spot, the expresso café, and of course we ordered our favorite drinks.

"How have you been, Shawntel?" I asked.

"I'm doing well, Savannah, and I owe it all to you. You've been that friend that every girl dreams of. I cannot thank you enough."

"Awe! That's what friends are for."

"Well, I have some good news for you," Shawntel said. "Chase and I have started dating, and so far it's been good. We're not going to rush things yet. We're starting off as friends. I'm not ready to be committed, and neither is he as of yet. Even though we know each other from the past. we drove separate cars to meet up. He wanted to pick me up, but I told him I'd drive instead and drive my car, and so I did just that. It's not like I didn't trust him. When I'm ready to go, I'll leave. We'll get to ride together one day just not right now. I know Chase, but I really want to get to know who he really is. I'm not getting into another relationship that has no meaning and is a waste of time. I've had enough of that. I'm looking more for companionship right now. If Chase is the man for me, then I'll be patient and protect my heart."

"Shawntel, there's nothing wrong with what makes you happy," I said. "You have to live it; no one else does. Now that you've been through the hurdles, you can live your life the way you choose. Choose happiness over fear. Happiness is knowing who you are, loving yourself, and definitely knowing your worth and finding peace. If you can't be number one in his life, then there's no reason to be number two. You are the girl who holds the key to every situation. Just take your time, and if it's meant to be, it will be. If not, it is what it is."

"Thank you, Savannah, for the encouraging words."

"Anytime!"

Everyone needs encouragement and motivation. It helps us get through the day. Life has its ups and downs, so we must be prepared to accept it or change it. You only live one time. So live it in a way that you will leave memories and a legacy that one will never forget. If a relationship is too perfect, then it's not real. You learn from the mistakes and try not to do it again. Someone who loves you the most will be the one who their heart shatters to pieces and still be there. You must protect your heart. Your heart plays a very important part of your feelings and makes tough decisions if you decide to ever have trust again. When you feel the need today again, you can't let your past relationship be a part of your future relationship. Every man or woman is not the same. It's ok to take a chance at love. Just make sure it's genuine.

Shawntel and Jorbin had not been communicating on coparenting. The alimony and child support hadn't stopped. Jorbin's fiancé must have been paying it because Jorbin did not have a job as what was told through the grapevine.

I received a call from an unknown number. It had been calling my number for about a week, but I never answered my phone due to all the unknown spam calls that I was receiving. I sent it straight to voicemail, which I never ever check. However, I noticed the same number called even after business hours, even at 11:00 p.m. at night. I kept saying, "I know darn well those spammers better not be calling me at this time of the night. They have one more time to call, and then I'm going to let them have a piece of my mind."

A couple of days went by, and I finally answered the call in a rude and sarcastic way. "Hello? I have so many bills to pay that if you're calling to pay them, I'll be glad to let you do so. Please STOP calling my phone."

"Ma'am, is this Savannah?"

"Yes it is, and what are you going to do about it?"

"Oh no, no, no, no—do not hang up! This is a very important call. This is Noretta, Jorbin's fiancé."

"How may I help you?" I said.

"I've been trying to get in touch with Shawntel to let her know that Jorbin had a stroke, and two weeks later he had a heart attack, but she's not answering," she said.

"And, ok?"

"I just wanted to let her know in case she is wondering why Jorbin hasn't called or picked the kids up."

"Oh, child please! Hell, before he was sick, the children never ever heard from their dad, so they don't know the difference anyway. But I will give Shawntel the message. Please send him my prayers!"

Before I reached out to Shawntel, I cooked dinner first. I cooked salmon over jasmine rice and broccoli. I served it with a glass of pinot grigio. After eating I took a nice, long relaxation spa bath. I did a facial. I went into my bedroom and turned on some smooth soul jazz on low volume. I poured me a second glass of wine, which was it for me. I am usually done with one, but I had had a very long day so a second glass was too much needed.

I called Shawntel. There was no answer so I sent her a text: "Good evening, best friend! When you get a chance, can you call me please? It is kind of urgent, but just whenever you get a chance. No rush, thank you!"

She was probably out with Chase or spending time with the kids. She would return my call. If she didn't call soon, she'd be talking to the voicemail.

After I finished up with this last glass of wine, I crashed and called it a good night. I knew it. As soon as I was on my way to bed, she finally called.

"Hey, girl, I called you," I said. "How are you?"

"I'm doing fine. Just got home. Chase and I were at the movies. We had such an amazing day. We went shopping, bought clothing for the kids, went to the movies, and out to dinner. He's been so good to me and the kids. I'm really starting to like him more and more. Savannah? What's going on with you, chick?"

"I'm well! I received a call from Jorbin's fiancé, Noretta. She said Jorbin had a stroke and a heart attack all within three weeks."

"Oh my God!" Shawntel said. "Did she say how he's doing?"

"She said he's ok!" I said.

"How did she get your number?"

"He must've had it, and she probably went through his phone. Who knows!"

"I'm going to tell the children. I don't want them to be upset right now. And besides he doesn't get the kids anyway, so it doesn't matter."

I said the same thing to Shawntel, but in a sense, I think it matters because when unexpected situations come, that's when we come to our senses. Those are his kids, and they deserve to know the truth. You see, we can't keep hiding the truth from children. But what we can do is educate them in the most positive way. That's how they grow up being honest, not only to others but with themselves.

"Yeah! You're right, Savannah. I will take the kids out to their favorite spot to the year-round food carnival. They love cotton candy and chili hot dogs, cotton candy, and candy apples. Their daddy will have an expensive dental bill," she laughed. "But of course it falls on me too! They love that place!"

"That's a great idea!" I said.

"It will be sweet but sad, but I'll make sure to let them know that everything will be all right. I expect my children to be honest with me, and I have to give them the same respect. Jorbin is not a bad father at all. We had our own problems because of his infidelity, and he couldn't control his lust for women. I was everything that Jorbin needed in a woman. I do understand that people fall out of love, but that's only if someone else has their attention. I can't blame or apologize for being myself, for being the woman that I've grown up to become. Maybe I wasn't enough of a woman for Jorbin."

"You gave birth to two beautiful children," I said. "Any woman who can carry a baby, deliver, struggle, work, pay bills, remain humbled, and take care of her man is astounding. You are a good woman. You were not built to break and not weak enough to fold. Whatever you're feeling or thinking I need for you to bounce back to reality, to the woman you have grown to love and to become.

"I know this is all overwhelming, and life can sometimes be unfair, but you can get through this. Troubles don't always last. I don't walk in your shoes and have experienced as much that you're going through but for some parts of my life. I've given up once upon a time, and I think that we all do. You have to learn how to let go at some point of time in your life."

"And I will, Savannah," she said. "It would take some time. Just keep me in your prayers please!"

"I will. I love you!"

"I love you too!"

You should never end your night mad or upset with anyone. You will toss and turn and have sleepless nights. Your thoughts will be lingering all over the place except for where they need to be. A good night's rest is very important, so when you wake up there's nothing that you're going to linger on to start off your new beginning.

I didn't upset Shawntel because I had so much respect for her and her well-being. She had a successful job and kids who she needed to focus on. Her mom had been very ill lately, so I did understand all that she was going through. When you love people, you give them peace and not pain. I do so much for Shawntel because she's my best friend, my sister, and my mentor as well. There were times when she had to coach me through college. I wanted to give up. She tutored me in some math classes. I could never get it right. I was making Cs, which was considered as a passing grade, and I was content with it. Shawntel would say, "No you can do better than that. And I'm going to make sure you get there."

And sure enough she got me there. I graduated with a 4.0. Thanks to her commitment, dedication and time. I was a case. I owe my life to her, and this is why I will forever be her mentor as well. We both may not be millionaires, billionaires, or *thousandaires*, but the friendship we have, money couldn't buy. We are our own harvest! We are doing the best we can with what we have. Like I stated before we may not always see eye to eye, but thank God we are not blind not to see the truth. When she's ready to talk, she will. I just give her the time and space that she needs. I never get into her personal life unless she tells me. I let her tell me when she's ready. And I respect her for that. She and I are much alike. When we don't want to be bothered, we will hibernate like the groundhog and only come out when it's time.

Shawntel was always a sweet girl. She was a tough girl growing up. When we were little, we used to set up a booth and sell food. Her grandpa, who was also my grandpa, was always getting on the two of us for not picking up pennies off the ground and putting them in the cookie jar. He was a man who used to save more coins than the bank itself. We used to play football with the boys in the street until the street-lights came on. And we knew it was time to come in when the streetlights came on. If we didn't, our parents would get a switch. After the first time we didn't obey, we got a whupping and ever since then as grown adults we've been in the house before mid-night. We met outside around 10:00 a.m. after we finished the chores around the house and set up our food stand. It was made out of wood and rocks, and we would sell hot pickles, sausages, pigs feet, hot boiled pickles, eggs, and Kool-Aid. The boys in the neighborhood wanted to get it free, and of course Shawntel didn't play that. She'd tell them, "Hell no." While I would always give them a sample. They had to buy or be gone. After we finished our sale for the day, which was about twenty six dollars a day, we were happy. I always wanted to go to the store. She wouldn't go for that. She used to say, "We have to save." I was the spender, and she was the saver. At the end of the day, our grandpa would make us come in, and Grandpa felt sorry for a neighborhood friend and let him stay. His name was Mitch. Mitch always stayed in the room smelling like peanuts and pee. The way the house was set up, his bedroom door was connected to Shawntel's, but there was a lock on it with a peep hole. We caught him doing nasty stuff to himself. He would drop peanuts through the hole to get our attention. We would peep through the hole, and he would slide his pants to the side so we could see his jolly rancher. He would do it on purpose. We ignored it for a little while, and then it started again. So we told our grandpa, and he put Mitch out!

One day we were in the room singing and dancing, and we decided to invite neighborhood friends named Polly and Deanna from across the street to come over so we could make up a dance routine. We were having so much fun until our neighborhood friend said she could dance better than one of our other best friends named Stephanie. Stephanie was around, but she was always playing basketball with the other neighborhood kids. But she was always a pro when it came to dancing.

I said, "Oh, no you can't."

Polly said, "Yes, I can!"

I got so angry that I body slammed her on the bed. At the time I weighed about 108 pounds, and she was about 160 pounds.

I told her, "Don't you ever say you could dance better than my friend." She ran home across the street crying. A month later we made peace. I'm the peacemaker, and Shawntel likes to negotiate. You don't stand a chance with her. She's definitely a tough one.

We would walk to the corner store not too far from Grandpa's house. I'd spend my whole ten dollars on two things, and she would look at me and say, "Are you crazy?"

"You just spent ten dollars on two things when you could have spent half of that and kept the remaining five dollars for later."

"Well, I'll worry about that later!"

She shook her head.

I wondered what kind of day it would be. I was sure whatever God had planned it would be productive. I guessed I'd reach out to my godchildren and take them to the beach. It was a beautiful day, and there was no need to be sitting in the house all day doing absolutely nothing. As I was driving, I was about to call Shawntel to let her know I was on the way to pick up my godchildren. Before I called her, my phone rang, and it was Shawntel. She was screaming out of control, and I couldn't understand what she was saying. I pulled over to the side of the road and tried to calm her down.

"Shawntel! Shawntel! What's wrong?"

"My mom died."

"What do you mean? What happened?"

At this point I was in total shock!

She was uncontrollably crying. "I had not heard from my mom in a week, and that was not like her not to check on me and the kids. I decided to drive over to her house where I had her key to get in and open the door, and she was on the floor with the cell phone next to her. I tried CPR. I checked her pulse, and there was no pulse! There was nothing! Nothing! Nothing! Nothing!"

Everything came as a shock and so fast. I couldn't tell Shawntel how to feel. All I could do was comfort and embrace her and continue to pray and love her. Dying is something we can't control. We don't know the time nor the day. We just have to prepare our families, love them more, create memories, and be there for each other as much as we possibly can. We are only on borrowed time. I try to spend as much time with my parents and siblings as possible. We can't stop what God has planned for us. I've lost my grandmother, aunts, uncles, and cousins. I've lost a very close special cousin who was like my best friend. She had a heart condition. She was so excited to get a heart transplant. She received it on her birthday. We celebrated a year later on her birthday, but after having the heart transplant, she passed away unexpectedly one year and twenty one days on her granddaughter's second birthday. And until this day, I hurt deep down in my soul. So I couldn't tell Shawntel how to feel. Everyone grieves differently.

She was ready to make plans for her mom's funeral; this is something no one wants to do, bury their loved ones. I did the obituaries, and Chase paid for all the flower arrangements. Her mother had life insurance, so that was taken care of. We just wanted to make sure her mom was beautiful and put her to rest peacefully.

Shawntel continued to grieve.

"Savannah, I don't believe all this is happening to me. First Jorbin and I divorced, now losing my mother. I've lost a job and a car all in the same breath. Sometimes I feel so mentally challenged, and I just want to give up!"

"Shawntel, you can't give up now," I said. "You have two beautiful children, and you have to keep living, to be here to love, support, and guide your children. They need you—I need you! You're not in this alone. Don't let them see you like this. I've told you before, we would never understand why life seems so unfair. Life is unfair to me at times, but I deal with it the best way I know how. I'm so sorry and saddened by all of this. Why don't you and the kids come over for dinner tonight?"

"Sure, we can do that!" Shawntel said. "Just know that my eyes will be swollen from crying."

"And I understand that," I said. "Do what you have to do. That's why we have tear ducts, to shed the pains or happiness. It's ok! I promise you! Would you be moving in with me as soon as we discussed a few weeks ago?"

"Of course, Savannah!"

"If you need anything—I mean anything, Shawntel— don't hesitate at all. We are all in this together, and I'll be darned if I let you go through this alone."

"I appreciate you so much, Savannah. You're the best."

A week passed by, and it was the day that we would bury Shawntel's mother. I prayed that God would please be with her and her children at this difficult time. Give her strength and comfort.

We arrived at the church where Mrs. Scott, Shawntel's mom, had been a member for forty-two years. Shawntel stepped out of the limousine, where she almost fainted, and Chase immediately embraced her and the kids, walking slowly into the church. Her children, Chase, and myself walked up to the casket and paid our respects and were seated. The remaining family and friends viewed and paid their respects, and then the casket was immediately closed for the service.

But just before the service started, Jorbin and Noretta arrived late. They both walked up to Shawntel asking if they could view Mrs. Scott and pay their final respects.

Shawntel's immediate response was, "NO! First of all, you walked in here late, which is very disrespectful. And second, you never respected my mom. So please go be seated before I have you removed from the premises."

Jorbin and Noretta proceeded to be seated.

Mrs. Scott was beautiful and laid to rest peacefully. Everything went well and smoothly. Shawntel held up really well. I think she accepted that her mom was no longer with us but in spirit.

At some point we all will break down from some sort of disappointment and shock. It is something that's called "life." No one is safe, perfect, or always has sunny days. Depends on what day it is and what comes our way. We just have to find a way for healing and the understanding of it all. Everything will not always be resolvable, but what we can do is try to eliminate the things that do not matter versus the things that do matter, which is separating what does not matter that causes the fire in our lives and put it out so that what matters in life, we can focus and pray about.

When it's time to start the healing process, we can move forward to getting strength and reclaiming life again, although the trials and tribulations that were once upon us have taught us a valuable lesson.

Shawntel and Chase had been dating for quite some time, and it was going really well for the both of them. I was so happy that she was reclaiming her life and regaining the strength and overcoming. She changed her hairstyle to a short, tapered cut, was dressing a little bit more sassy and classy, and she's was definitely changing her eating habits. Chase had been introducing her to other cultures and foods. That was something she really needed. She was definitely living the life that she deserved. He was definitely filling the voids that she had with all that she had been through. This was the guy she should have married a long time ago. He was such an awesome guy and definitely a keeper.

I wanted her to spend as much time as she needed with Chase. The only time I reached out to her was to be sure she was ok and to see if she and the kids needed anything. She assured me that they were doing just fine.

It felt so good knowing my loved one was doing well and regaining her hopefulness. I felt like I was walking on clouds and not falling through them. I could finally get some rest. I am the type that my brains don't shut off. My brain is like a clock; it just keeps on working nonstop unless it has some human removable batteries to stop it from overthinking.

Noretta and Jorbin decided to get married. On their wedding day, they had a live taping of their wedding. As Noretta was walking down the altar aisle, Jorbin was so emotional with teardrops rolling down the side of his face like he was the happiest man in the world. As Noretta got closer to her fiancé, she had this evil smile on her face, but you couldn't tell if that was just how she looked or if she was just the evil person who she was because that was just how she looked. When a bride walks down the aisle, you don't know her motives or what she's thinking or her emotional feelings. As the pastor read the vows, Jorbin said, "I do," but when it was Noretta's turn, she said, "I don't!" Everyone was shocked and stunned, thinking it was a joke. And it was absolutely not! She said, "I care about you and everything, and I love you but not in a way to take care of you financially, mentally, physically, and even to death do us part."

Whoa! Wow!

At this point watching the public live video, we were thinking, "Ok, this is just a joke." But she immediately took off her rings, placed them in Jorbin's hands and walked off. He stood there in an unbelievable state of mind. She left the altar, got into her limousine, and didn't look back twice, and she immediately left. She didn't give the guests any notice; she didn't apologize or thank them for coming.

A few months later, Jorbin decided to stay with Noretta to see if he could win her back. Shawntel was out on a date with her fiancé at the steak and grill restaurant. She sent me a text message that Noretta and Jorbin were there, and they were seated at the next available table. Shawntel and her fiancé were enjoying each other, talking, laughing, holding hands, embracing each other, and just being in love and happy when all of a sudden she heard continuously coughing. She looked over and it was Jorbin. At the same time Shawntel thought he had a cough, but he kept pointing and holding his throat, thinking Noretta was going to ask him if he was ok. She didn't! She kept telling him to drink water and eat slowly. Shawntel immediately rushed out of her chair and started doing the Heimlich maneuver on Jorbin. He had been choking on a piece of steak. Noretta sat there like she had no care in the world. That was because she knew Jorbin had her on his life insurance policy as the beneficiary, or so she thought. What she failed to realize was that he had removed her and added Shawntel as the beneficiary if something happened to him to make sure his children were taken great care of.

There is absolutely no way that I would be in a desperate need to be in a relationship if I was standing up at my wedding in front of a live taping and choking and still be with a spiteful woman. If this didn't get his attention that Noretta didn't want him, then I didn't know what else needed to happen to get attention.

Now I'll talk about I'd been doing with my life. A friend of mine reached out to ask if I wanted to go to the NBA Lakers game. At the time I said, "No!" With all that I had going on with my best friend, there was no way I would be able to enjoy myself. Once I knew she was moving in a positive way and slowly healing, I planned to call him back and see if those tickets were still up for grabs and if so, heck yeah! I was taking him up on that offer.

I called him back, and we talked on the phone for a little while, and sure thing I accepted the invite. All I had to do was get my Lakers gear and clothing gear together and have a blast. I didn't have to pay for anything. We had separate beds that he booked. We had front row seats. He must've paid some money for those front row tickets. But I wasn't the one to complain, honey! I was not mad at all—up close and personal with the celebs—that was right up my alley. He told me to come as I was. And why did he say that? I sure would!

Jonathan was much different than the other guy I'd dated. He was definitely a keeper. He was not disrespectful at all. This one guy I dated was just horrible all the way around. I would just lie there and watch the paint dry on the wall. He was just that lame. I continued the relationship out of boredom and hoping it would get better, but it didn't. He was very aggressive and rude, and that didn't work for me. His kisses were not romantic or meaningful.

His lovemaking skills were offbeat and unbalanced. I had to teach him, and I didn't like that. He was just all over the place. A grown man should never have to be educated about how to please a woman. I couldn't deal with him anymore. He swore he was the man. Absolutely NOT! I let him do it, but just not with me. I thank God every day for my protected peace. I don't mind letting go of a can of dry paint. No matter what the color is.

It was a rainy day, and it was a good time to just chill at home and relax and enjoy some me time. It was about 9:30 p.m., and of course you know me, I was about to get a snack and wind down. It had been a long day. I'd been very positive, motivated, and productive, and I would not complain at all. As I was sitting there, thoughts were going through my mind as to why being married was so important and what was the big deal? I guess if both were dedicated in love, honesty, respect, and loyalty, then it was definitely worth the while. Diamonds would come only in time. If one feeling was opposite than the other, and if it wasn't mutual, then it wasn't going to work. That was the scenario in my past relationship. I would never settle for less than or anything. I controlled my feelings and thoughts, I protected my heart, and I definitely protected my peace.

The sun doesn't always shine twice a day. It will give you one good, bright day, and it's up to you to continue to shine and have a stress-free day. If the sun is shining, and the skies are blue, be grateful for the simplest things that God has given you. Glow, smile, and shine like the sun until the sunset. Even after the sunset, you should see yourself just as beautiful, unified, unique, and beautiful as ever.

On this beautiful Sunday morning, I decided not to attend Sunday morning church services. I just want to take some time alone and just relax. Maybe I'd go to the gym, do some cardio work, and then stop by the market and pick up some fresh berries, kale, and spinach. Then stop by the seafood market and pick up some fresh, pink salmon, which reminded me—I was low on wine, and you know that's a big no no!

Shawntel had this little itty-bitty dog named Sasha. She knew how I felt about dogs no matter how big or small a dog was. I am just terrified of them. She always told me, "Oh, hush. My little baby is not going to bother you. She just wants to play."

In my mind I'm like, "Yeah ahhh, little itty-bitty Sasha is evil. She likes to jump on me and bite on my pantleg and eat my shoe." When I would go to Shawntel's house, I would wear steel-toed boots. Shawntel would get a kick out of it. I didn't like that, and Shawntel would just laugh. But there's a story behind why I do not like and trust dogs.

After school one day, we were walking home and decided to stop by her cousin's house to grab a snack. We opened the gate to enter, and this big white dog named Bingo was charging at us. Shawntel ran out of the gate and locked it, and she left me there with Bingo. He came running after me, latching onto my skirt and not letting go. I was running and screaming until her cousin heard the commotion. Shawntel stood outside the gate laughing and yelling, "Bingo let go of her dress, you naughty dog you. Let go of her dress right now!" And so he did. Her cousin said, "Bingo likes to play."

I was shaking, and I haven't been right since. Until this day she and I get a kick out of it, and I have not been back to her cousin's house since then. The only dog I'll get close to is a cute little Yorkie. Other than that, no thank you! Nothing can convince me that all dogs just want to play.

"Shawntel, are you up to going bowling tonight?" I said. "I guess I'll forgive you."

"Sure! Let me see what Chase wants to do, or if he has anything planned for me and the kids. I will get back with you and let you know later this afternoon."

I loved the communication between her and Chase. Before she made any decision or commitment to anything, she made sure she and Chase had nothing planned. They both had great communication and respect for each other. I was happy to know that she and Chase were starting their relationship off the healthy way. She'd been through so much, and the last thing I needed was for her to be unhappy. She deserved nothing but love and respect, which is priceless.

Shawntel and Chase discussed, and they had nothing planned, so we decided to go bowling. The kids, Serenity and Isaiah, were just as excited as I was. None of us could bowl, but we were going to do our best. It was all about family fun. We got to the bowling alley, and of course all the size six and one-half shoes were gone. I decided to put on a size eight. I was flip-flopping around like they were house slippers, but I made it work. Serenity and Isaiah found their correct sizes, and with Shawntel's big foot— she wears a size nine—there were plenty of bowling shoes available.

I bowled for an hour or so. I was not winning at all. I couldn't beat the kids. I sat down, and of course you know me, they had a snack and wine bar. I went straight to the wine bar and purchased one glass of wine. I didn't want to overdo it because I had to drive. Shawntel was not winning at all. She joined me on the bench to have a glass of wine too. We sat there and watched the kiddos have a good time. Serenity and Isaiah were doing great.

Serenity was ten years old. She was such a sporty girl. She was always in the spotlight. She was very smart, outgoing, and funny. She was very playful and always cheerful and joyful. She was on the tumble team and swim team. She was very athletic and cheered for her brother's football team. Her cheer coach made her lead captain. You could hear her mouth across town. She loved acting, singing and dancing and wanted to be a director in acting and someday be on the usher board in the church.

She reminded me of her mom though. She loved helping others. One time a homeless man was sleeping on the sidewalk, and it was a hot day. Serenity wanted us to stop and give him her ice cream.

She asked me, "Tee Tee Treasure, can we buy him some ice cream?"

"Sure Serenity!" We turned around and went to the store, and I told Serenity to pick out the kind she thought the homeless man would like.

She came back with a gallon of rainbow (chocolate, strawberry, and vanilla) ice cream.

I said, "Serenity, what are you doing sweetheart? He can't eat all that ice cream. It will melt. How do you know he likes that kind?"

"Well Tee Tee Treasure, think of it this way, he can share with his other homeless friends, and that's why he has different flavors. He can just scoop out which one he likes the best."

I turned around and minded my business and paid for it. She definitely told me!

I thought she had what it took to do and be whatever she wanted. She would be successful at it. She also wanted to be committed to her church—on the children's usher board and choir. This little girl was ambitious.

Isaiah was a handsome eleven-year-old kid. He knew what was right and what was wrong. He was the type of kid who sometimes had emotions that could be up and down because he just wanted his father in his life, and he wanted to always be like his father but, he said, in a more positive way. He was smart and generous, and he loved his mama. He liked to be the big helper around the house since his dad had been gone. He loved and respected Chase. Chase took him fishing on the boat. He helped his mom bring the groceries in the house. He comforted and embraced her when he knew she was not feeling well or she was upset about something. He was just this eleven-year-old kid who had a big heart.

He was not the type of kid who was all hype about video games. He liked to read, fix things, loved cars, and he had always told his mama that one day he would build her a home. He was definitely athletic. He played football and basketball. In fact he was the runner of the football. He enjoyed soccer from time to time, but he said it was no fun—that it was like playing kickball. He was the type of kid that would definitely tell you what he liked and what he did not like.

He and his sister were very close, and he was very protective of her. It was good to see siblings who loved and protected one another. It was a beautiful thing. He was a good kid and Shawntel never had any problems out of him.

As Shawntel and I sat back, sipping on our wine and watching the kids continue to bowl and have such a wonderful time, she looked over at me and said, "I'm so thankful for our friendship. I couldn't ask for a better friend. I'm thankful for you, Savannah. I'm so full and ready to go. Let's get the kids packed up and stop by a burger joint and get the kids something to eat. There's nothing here they will like. I need to get them settled and go cuddle and spend time with my man."

"Ok then Ms. Stella Got Her Groove Back," I said, both of us chuckling.

I finally made it back home after a long and beautiful evening with my bestie and my godchildren. We had such a wonderful time. I thanked God for his grace and the safe travels back.

I think it's so important to keep moving in the right direction of where God takes you. You can never go wrong. If so you did not follow the steps that you were led to.

Shawntel and I went to church faithfully. We'd always prayed together no matter what situation, the good or the bad. Her mom was the first lady of the church until her husband passed away. He was the pastor. Mrs. Scott was a very beautiful and dedicated woman. I saw that in Shawntel and Serenity. Even though Shawntel and I had busy schedules, we still made time for the Lord.

My phone rang, and of course it was my best friend who called to tell me that Chase asked her to marry him and she had said yes!

"I'm so excited for you," I said. "I'm so happy you didn't give up on love and, most importantly, on yourself."

"I know, Savannah. We have to take a risk on everything we do in life, and if it doesn't work, it's just not meant to be. I would just move on. Hold on, Savannah, my phone is beeping, and it's Jorbin's fiancé, Noretta. I wonder what she wants?"

Shawntel answered the phone.

"Hi, Shawntel, this is Noretta. I called to tell you that Jorbin had another heart attack, and I'm going to place him in a nursing home where he can get the care he needs. I can't keep putting my life on hold when my life is going well. He's stopping my blessings. and I can't receive it at 100 percent because I'm too busy taking care of him, and I don't have the time.

"Can you make sure he's in a caring, clean, safe, and nice environment?" Shawntel said. "You do know he still deserves proper care, and he's the father of my kids. He's a brother, friend, and a son? I can give him that much respect. He's still my kid's father regardless."

"Look, Shawntel, he doesn't have much income coming in," Noretta said. "He's going to a nursing home according to his budget, and that's very slim to none."

"Noretta, though he's your fiancé, he left me for you. The least you could do is make sure he's in good hands and comfortable."

"Shawntel, your kids can do all that when they get older. Right now he's going to the nursing facility of my choice."

"You're so spiteful, Noretta. Don't ever call my phone again!"

"Oh my God, Savannah, that was Noretta," Shawntel said. "Jorbin had another heart attack, and she's going to put him in a nursing facility because she doesn't have time for him."

"Are you serious?"

"Yes!"

"I'm at a loss for words," I said. "I will let you go so you can talk with the children and Chase to let them know what's going on. Lord have mercy, this is a mess."

This is what happens when you think grass is greener on the other side. Jorbin had a good loving and caring wife. He allowed his lust to control his life. I was sure he'd think twice before doing others wrong.

But in his condition, I didn't think he'd ever get the woman he deserved. He really needed to take good care of his health before getting in any relationship at the moment. My sincere prayers were with him through all this.

Noretta was done with Jorbin and placed him in a nursing facility. Shawntel wouldn't hear too much from her. I was hoping his nearest relative would reach out to her for the sake of the kids. He wanted to see his kids more than ever before. There is nothing more precious than spending time and loving your kids before your became terminally ill, disabled, or even while you're in good health. When your time expires, there's no coming back. I was proud of his kids for doing the right thing and not seeing him in a negative way, and that they had moved on from the past.

Two years into their relationship, Shawntel and Chase finally got married at the courthouse. It was beautiful. The children I were there to witness the beautiful ceremony.

I was the planner and the host for the reception. I rented a venue that had a bar, a DJ area, an open dance floor, and a kitchen. I did all the catering and paid for the venue, purchased all the foods and drinks, sent out invitations, and decorated in turquoise and white. I didn't want Shawntel lifting a finger and doing anything. It was beautiful. She and Chase had no clue of the surprise wedding reception. I surprised both of them, and they had the surprise of their lives. The cake was a three-layer pound cake inside with cream cheese filling, decorated in the colors of turquoise and white. There were sixty-two guests. Serenity and Isaiah had a blast. In fact they had some little cousins and friends running around there too! They loved everything about Chase, and he loved them as his own.

The reception ended around 10:30 p.m. I was going to get my money's worth. There were no food, drinks, or anything left at all. The photographer was on time and took a lot of memories. I had to pray that everything went well, and it did. I hadn't seen my best friend that happy in a long time.

Since Chase was finishing up his masters of arts in religion to become a pastor, I kept the music mindful and respectful. But he also had a blast.

Jorbin and Noretta were invited. However, Noretta did show up but not with Jorbin; instead she brought another man. I politely turned her around.

"No, ma'am. You're not coming up here being disrespectful, young lady." And so she did leave. She was no longer welcome to anything after the way she treated Jorbin, and that was very disrespectful to the kids. He was my godkids' father, and she would not walk up in there like nothing ever happened.

Three months into Shawntel and Chase's marriage, Chase decided to have a discussion with Shawntel about providing additional assistance to help him. They decided to move Jorbin to an upscale nursing facility that rated all five stars. Jorbin did accept and sign the agreement. Chase would pay the nursing facility an additional $1,300 per month so he could get the care that he needed. Chase did not want his stepkids to see the way their father was going to be living. He loved those kids as his own. Shawntel definitely had a winning husband. I supported and respected their decision. That was the best gift a person could get from an ex-wife who was married to a pastor. I don't think there's any better gift—the love and support from Shawntel and Chase one could ever receive from a beautiful, loving and delightful couple.

Chase was planning to build a church welcoming religious, habitual worshippers, and a praying congregation. Shawntel would be Mrs. first lady. I couldn't wait and I was excited to be a part of a new and uplifting congregation, which I knew I would fit in perfectly with—a lot of love, praise, and worship.

I had lost my pastor about one year ago to an illness. Things had not been quite the same for me. I'd learned to manage it slowly, wanting to join a more welcoming not-all-about-dress-code type of congregation. I'd searched and visited many congregations. But the Lord told me to hold on, he had something even better.

I was sure Chase and Shawntel's church would be family oriented and welcoming. I would be engaged in a church that would be drama-free and a worthy place to serve an Almighty God.

I was on my way to pick up my godchildren and take them shopping because they had gotten report cards, and they'd been through so much. They deserved a trip to Florida to Disney World. They had no idea. This was definitely going to be a surprise

I told them to pack their bags, and whatever they didn't have, we'd purchase it along the way. Shawntel knew about the trip all along, so she was part of the plan as well.

Four hours into the drive the kids want to stop at Build-A-Burger to build a burger the way they wanted it. Build-A-Burger is a place for kids. But of course adults too—withI whatever topping you desire to build your burger.

After we purchased our Build-A-Burgers, we were eating, singing, and just enjoying our ride. All of a sudden, an eighteen-wheeler pulled out in front of us and hit Serenity's side, crushing the right back seat.

I yelled, "No, no, no. Serenity! Serenity!" Nothing from Serenity.

Isaiah was freaking out crying for help!

The ambulance arrived four minutes later. The paramedics removed Serenity from the car, performing CPR over and over again. Still no signs of life. Serenity had a slight pulse but passed on the way to the hospital.

The hardest thing I had to ever do in my life was to make that phone call to my best friend and tell her what had happened. It had torn me apart to the core of my soul. I knew she was going to hate me for life.

I called Shawntel crying nonstop. I could not control myself. "We just got into a horrible, tragic accident, and Serenity did not make it," I said. "Lord please bring her back."

"What do you mean Serenity did not make it? My child is gone? What do you mean Serenity didn't make it, Savannah?"

"The truck hit her side, and she passed. The paramedics did everything to try and save her."

Shawntel dropped the phone and started screaming.

"I'm so sorry!" I said. "I'm so sorry!"

The cry that Shawntel cried was so indescribable.

She flew immediately to be by her daughter's side.

Isaiah remained in the hospital with whiplash and shock.

Shawntel made arrangements to have her daughter sent back to Georgia, where she would have the funeral.

We both sat quietly on our way back to Georgia. She didn't say a word to me, and I couldn't blame her.

She tried to open the plane door to jump out. We got up quickly to stop her. She screamed and cried. She was in so much pain. I was in so much pain because had I not taken the kids to Disney World then Serenity would have still been alive. I blamed myself for it all. I would never forgive myself even as

I was speaking to Shawntel and was trying to calm her down. We both were in a terrible state of mind.

"It was something terrible that I will never forget, and I am so sorry," I said. "I am so sorry, Shawntel."

"I'm not blaming you, Savannah," she said. "I know it's not your fault. All of this has taken me by surprise. I know Serenity did not suffer. She loved and had a good life. She's in heaven taking care of the angels of God's children. She is with the Lord now and with her grandmother. I have to accept it. We are all here just for a moment. And I know she's in good hands. I now have to live with my one and only child, Isaiah. I have to be strong for him. I know God would never leave us nor forsake us. I have a faithful and praying husband who I know will make sure we're in good hands. I must put my child to rest now. God give me the strength and please keep Jorbin in your prayers, as he's going through his own battles now losing his only daughter. I promise I will make sure Serenity lives on forever. She was such a beautiful, inspiring, and bright little girl. She was my heartbeat, my life, my love, my Queen, she was my everything. Savannah, would you pray for the healing of my only son?"

"Sure, Shawntel!"

"Lord, we trust in you. We ask for restoration, healing, and a speedy recovery for Isaiah. I believe in your will that his mind, body, and spirit will be restored and covered. I trust in you and I believe in you that in your power that it will be done. In Jesus's name I pray, Amen."

Amen!

Oh how it brought so much joy and tears to Shawntel, knowing that she was a very strong woman. After everything that she had been through, she was still standing. She said, "God is not finished with me yet, as I still have work to do on earth."

I was so happy that Shawntel was living and not giving up. There is always light at the end of the tunnel. I was so happy that she was still my friend after all of this. Even with the struggles I'd been through she would always say, "You got this!"

Although life can turn for the worst, each of us will experience some type of trials and tribulations, heartaches, and pains of losing loved ones. We all are only here temporarily. We have to learn to love, learn to heal, and forgive again.

Four months after Serenity's passing, Shawntel and Chase built a new church in Florida, and named it after Serenity. Serenity Faith, Healing and Hope Church.

The school she attended was named in her honor, Serenity's Christian Academy.

Chase and Shawntel's church in Florida, Serenity Faith and Hope Church, has touched so many lives that the congregation has grown bigger. Serenity, Faith and Hope Church was expanded to California, Georgia, and Michigan. I was given the opportunity to receive my degree in theology and am now ministering in Michigan.

For we are not in this alone. Whatever religion you believe in, I hope it's a religion that brings you life, comfort, sympathy, love, power, hope, peace, and forgiveness. Nothing is easy in life, and we can't expect for everything to be easy. Life will take us for a run of a lifetime, but it's up to us to know how to take it and how to run with it. Everything that we go through may look easy to the strong ones, but even the strong ones get weak, tired, and hurt too. It's a part of life, a part of the process, and a plan to better prepare ourselves for the possibilities that shall arise. We may never know how the storm would hit us differently. We have to be prepared, take shelter, and accept what it is because the storm shall pass. The skies may be blue, and there may be sunny days; never take life for granted. Don't leave this world without making peace. Don't let a small misunderstanding that is petty and can be resolved make you miss out on your season that God has created to be your destiny, your blessings, and your peace. Live each day like it's your last day, love unconditionally like you've never loved before, and pray because prayer changes things.

I've decided to stay with my husband after thirty years of marriage. After all we have been through with finances, trust issues, and relationships with others, they were just petty things that we should have been able to communicate on, but we didn't at the time. We've reconciled our differences, forgiven each other, prayed and meditated together, and rebuilt our unity. Living happily ever after!

The more challenges we go through in our lives, the better we become and see the light.

The troubles we face are all a part of learning you can't give up on those who are worried and concerned.

We hide behind a cold and dark shadow.

We should be praying to God to make it better.

Without the trials and tribulations in our lives, how could we survive without knowing why?

Define the problems and fix it fast; troubles don't always last.

It will get better with the days ahead and months to come; we must keep our head up until it's all done.

We make decisions when the time is right, so don't rush into something you don't like.

Be patient in all that you do.

Remember no one has to live that life but you.

Choosing faith over fears leaves space for healing, dreams, and opportunities.

Milton Keynes UK
Ingram Content Group UK Ltd.
UKHW021933211124
451398UK00008B/348

9 798822 956520

.